Alvin

the Zookeeper

Alvin
the Zookeeper

By Ulf Löfgren

Carolrhoda Books, Inc./Minneapolis

One day when Alvin was out walking he came to a zoo. I bet *lots* of animals are in there, he thought to himself.

A zookeeper. Now there's something I wouldn't mind being, reflected Alvin. I like all kinds of animals: monkeys, elephants, tigers, lions, bears, giraffes. Why I even like frogs. At least I *think* I do . . . .

Just then a door opened right next to Alvin, and a man stuck his head out.

"He's here," shouted the man to someone inside. "The new keeper is here."

Then he said to Alvin, "Come on in."

"Good to have you here at last" said the zoo manager. "You can begin right away by feeding the animals. But do not let any of them out of the zoo. The animals are always talking about it. They'd like to get out if they could. But that's forbidden. Absolutely forbidden!"

The zoo manager gave Alvin a keeper's cap and a special badge to pin on his shirt.

"Feed the animals, but remember what I told you. *Do not* let them out of the zoo," said the manager again.

Alvin went to feed the bears first.

"We'd just love to go on a little trip somewhere," the bears said eagerly to Alvin.

"Couldn't you help us get out into the country,
just once?"

Then Alvin took food to the seals.

"Look Alvin," said the seals, "there's one thing we'd like to do very, very much. We'd like to see a bit of the world. Can you help us?"

"Alvin," whispered the monkeys, "can't you arrange for us to go somewhere and have a little fun?"

"Well, I don't know," replied Alvin. "The manager said it's not allowed!"

"This is really tasty," said the giraffe, when he was given a twig of fresh green leaves. "But do you know what we'd like more than anything else? We'd like to get out of here, just for a single day."

The penguins also gathered around Alvin and wanted to talk to him. "You there, Alvin. Please help us go on a holiday in the countryside."

Now all the animals flocked around Alvin.
"Please Alvin," they said, "surely you can fix it
so that we can take a trip to some nice little lake.
We *promise* that we won't run away."

"Do you *really* promise?" asked Alvin.

"We promise. We promise," they all said as sincerely
as they could.

Surely they should be allowed a visit to the country
just once, thought Alvin to himself. But I
wonder what the manager
would say . . . ?

So one night when the moon shone brightly, Alvin led all the animals out of the zoo. "Shhhhhhh," he whispered. "You must promise me two things: keep very quiet and don't eat each other up. Eat the food in your picnic baskets instead."

"We promise, we promise," murmured all the animals.

"Walk quietly then," said Alvin. "No scuttling, or shuffling, or stamping."

All night long the animals walked and trotted out into the countryside. Just as the morning sun came up, they arrived at a lovely lake beside a beautiful meadow.

"We'll stop here," called Alvin. "You can swim in the lake and play in the meadow."

The animals thought this was a splendid idea!

What a glorious time they all had. They ate up all the good things they had in their baskets, because they had become very hungry after that long walk in the moonlight.

Then they played together all day, swinging, throwing balls, playing hide-and-seek, rushing down the slide, and squirting and splashing water on each other. They had never in their lives had so much fun and had never been on such a wonderful trip!

But back at the zoo, the manager was pacing back and forth. He ran around and around when he discovered that the animals were gone!

"What on earth has happened! The rhinoceros is gone," he exclaimed. "And so is the giraffe and the elephant!"

"Am I going crazy? The bears
are gone too, all of them! And
so are the monkeys, and the
moose, and the camel, and the
tiger, and the hippopotamus!
I must be going out of my mind!"
Then the manager threw himself
into a heap on the ground.

When evening came, Alvin told the animals it
was time to go back to the zoo. "Be very quiet,"
whispered Alvin, "so that nobody will hear us."
Even the elephants tried to walk silently.

The next day the animals were all back in their
cages when the manager showed up.

"But, but . . . they were all gone yesterday," muttered
the manager. "I'm absolutely, definitely, positively
certain that they were gone yesterday."

"Maybe," said Alvin, "you only dreamed the animals
were gone. Today they are here right before your eyes."

"But now I've got to get going," Alvin said quickly. "It's hard work being a zookeeper. But great fun too!"

This edition first published 1991 by Carolrhoda Books, Inc.
Originally published by Norstedts Förlag, Stockholm.
Original edition copyright © 1990 by Ulf Löfgren under the title
Albin Djurskötare.

Library of Congress Cataloging-in-Publication Data

Löfgren, Ulf
  [Albin djurskötare. English]
  Alvin the Zookeeper / by Ulf Löfgren.
      p.   cm.
  Translation of: Albin djurskötare.
  Summary: Young Alvin lets the animals out of the zoo for a
lovely picnic, and no one eats anyone else or runs away.
    ISBN 0-87614-689-2
    [1. Zoo animals—Fiction. 2. Zoos—Fiction. 3. Picnicking—
Fiction.] I. Title.
PZ7.L826Alh 1991
[E]—dc20   91-9638
                                                                  CIP
                                                                   AC

Manufactured in the United States of America
1 2 3 4 5 6 7 8 9 10 00 99 98 97 96 95 94 93 92 91